This book belongs to

....

For Terry—L. M.

SIMON & SCHUSTER BOOKS FOR YOUNG READERS
An imprint of Simon & Schuster Children's Publishing Division
1230 Avenue of the Americas, New York, New York 10020
Text copyright © 2015 by Mark Sperring
Illustrations copyright © 2015 by Layn Marlow
Originally published in 2015 in Great Britain by Oxford University Press
SIMON & SCHUSTER BOOKS FOR YOUNG READERS
is a trademark of Simon & Schuster, Inc.
For information about special discounts for bulk purchases,
please contact Simon & Schuster Special Sales at
1–866–506–1949 or business@simonandschuster.com.
The Simon & Schuster Speakers Bureau can bring authors to your
live event. For more information or to book an event, contact
the Simon & Schuster Speakers Bureau at 1–866–248–3049
or visit our website at www.simonspeakers.com.
The text for this book is set in Langtry WF.
The illustrations for this book are rendered digitally.
Manufactured in China
0319 OUP
First Simon & Schuster Books for Young Readers paperback edition June 2019
2 4 6 8 10 9 7 5 3 1
CIP data for this book is available from the Library of Congress.
ISBN 978–1–4814–5206–9 (hardcover)
ISBN 978–1–5344–5209–1 (pbk)
ISBN 978–1–4814–5207–6 (eBook)

I'll Catch You
If You Fall

Written by Mark Sperring
Illustrated by Layn Marlow

Simon & Schuster Books for Young Readers
New York   London   Toronto   Sydney   New Delhi

Who will keep the boy safe?

"I will," said his mother.

"I will hold him close . . .

and never let him lean too far. "

But who will keep
them both safe?

"Me," said the captain.

"I will steer the boat

and keep a watch."

But who will keep the boat safe?

"I will,"
        said the star.

"I will guide the boat
over the foaming waves,

and through the storm . . .

into the little harbor . . .

and all the way home.

"But who will keep me safe?"
asked the star.

"I will," said the boy.

"I will lean out my window,

but not too far . . .

and

catch

you

if

you

fall."

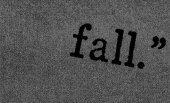